RELATIONSHIPPING

THE KEY TO CORPORATE VALUE

George Wiedemann

To order additional copies of this book, contact:
Xlibris
1-888-795-4274
www.Xlibris.com
Orders@Xlibris.com

ISBN: Softcover   978-1-7960-9447-3
         EBook   978-1-7960-9446-6

Print information available on the last page

Rev. date: 03/13/2020

CHAPTERS

FOREWORD

To succeed these days in engaging customers with the brand and its enterprise, thereby increasing enterprise value, the C-suite must deal with understanding the disruption brought about by technology in the marketing world.

To deliver on objectives and to address the changes involved in winning and serving customers, the C-suite team needs to realign the art and science of engaging consumers with brands. Operationalizing adaptation to the new consumer behaviors will focus the full power of martech science and art to build the customer base and enterprise value.

We are living through a time of transformation brought about by Internet connectivity, online technology, personal devices and all those digital interactions that are daily moving engagement away from the still-robust world of offline communication interactions. With connectivity, consumer behavior has dramatically changed.

That this disruption of engagement is not uniform across generations only complicates matters. To a great extent, Baby Boomers have adapted to technology, but it's hardly surprising that older populations still prefer doing business the "old" way — in offline channels with traditional behaviors. Meanwhile, the Generation X and Millennial populations have gone deeply digital but still embrace offline channels. Generation Z (and younger) grew up plugged in; therefore, engaging that cohort is uniquely and dominantly digital.

To use a hockey metaphor, it's important to skate to where the puck is going — not where it is now. That's why I suggest that, given the speed of digital and technological transformation, the movement of attention to digital platforms, and the birth of big data, we need to adopt a new way of bonding the customer to the brand.

We need to embrace customer-centricity by examining management silos and solutions to unify all touchpoints into a superior brand experience. In order to do so, it's essential that we master digital connectivity. Consumers today want to engage in a relationship with the brand — one that's personal and robust.

C H A P T E R   1

RELATIONSHIPPING IS OVERTAKING MARKETING

To succeed today in cultivating a brand's user loyalty, in growing brand revenue and returns and ultimately in expanding enterprise value, we need to change four things: our approach, strategy, execution and terminology.

We need to move away from marketing, which is being overtaken by the current technology revolution in which we are immersed. Given that the consuming world is largely a *connected* world, with consumers connected to brands and their products through mobile devices, laptops and desktops, I believe that we need to create a new name — and a new paradigm — for our initiative: relationshipping. And we need to apply it as a new way of thinking in our efforts to move goods and services.

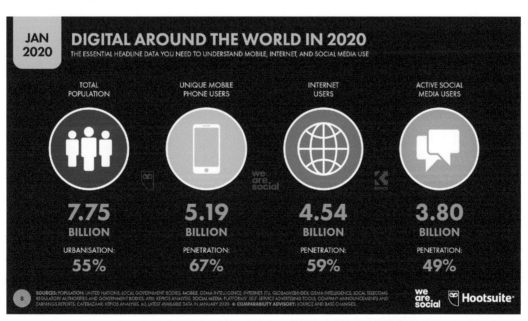

Source: https://wearesocial.com/blog/2020/01/
digital-2020-3-8-billion-people-use-social-media

Relationshipping is the art and science of bonding the consumer to the brand digitally, with the final metric focus on generating optimum customer lifetime value (CLV). Achieving this goal requires grounding in data and technology, which together support brand personalization. Relationshipping is a fundamentally customer-centric enterprise, and is consummated across various Moments of Truth (MOTs). In the 21st century, winning new customers and fostering relationships begins at the Zero Moment of Truth: (ZMOT). Let's take a look at how martech has impacted these moments.

Jan Carlzon introduced the Moment of Truth approach in the 1980s. In his estimation, any contact with the product and brand constituted "truth" and contributed to a consumer forming a mindset about the brand. In 2005, A.G. Lafley, Chairman, President and CEO of Procter & Gamble, presented his own version(s).

- **First Moment of Truth** (FMOT): P&G describe it as the moment a consumer chooses a product over the other competitor's offerings. My favorite way of thinking of this was shared with me by my first agency boss, Lester Wunderman. After seeing our ads, the FMOT happens in the store aisle when the consumer selects our product on the shelf — not the competitor's product 12 inches away. *Today, this happens two ways: in the marketplace, or online (via the website or social media).*
- **Second Moment of Truth** (SMOT): This interaction occurs (and re-occurs) whenever the consumer uses the product.
- **Third Moment of Truth** (TMOT): This moment involves everything the consumer says about the brand to others in the household, as well as to friends and family. *I would add that this moment expands in the connected world by the experience sharing — e.g., the consumer posting reviews on purchasing sites and comments in social media conversations. Also, brands harness the Third Moment by organizing brand advocates to publish a continuous stream of advice and praise about the brand.*

A fourth Moment was added by Google in 2011.

- **Zero Moment of Truth** (ZMOT) is the micro-moment in which the prospect or customer has demand or need for a product or service, and plugs key words into the search bar — particularly at any of four primary sites for this activity: Google, Bing, Facebook and Amazon. Staying with the P&G thinking, this means that, when a consumer types "laundry detergent" into the search field, the Tide brand manager wants "Tide" to appear at the top of the page, not "Cheer." *According to research conducted by Google, 88% of US customers research online before actually buying the product.*

For relationshipping, the most important of these interactions is the Zero Moment. Beginning at that point, relationshipping is the process by which the brand engages with the consumer to forge a digital relationship and build customer lifetime value (CLV), which in turn builds the brand and drives enterprise value.

Bottom line: We need to stop thinking of the process of selling stuff or services as beginning at the market (or website) where the product or service sits, then using PR and advertising to drive people there. As a concept, marketing was born centuries ago in an *unconnected* world. The word "marketing" came into being when goods were first assembled in a gathering place for people to go and shop.

A quick review of Wikipedia points us toward the word's origins: "According to etymologists, the term 'marketing' first appeared in dictionaries in the sixteenth century, where it referred to the process of buying and selling at a market. The contemporary definition of 'marketing' as a process of moving goods from producer to consumer with an emphasis on sales and advertising first appeared in dictionaries in 1897."

Not only is the construct of marketing old, it's also been largely altered. All the "Five Ps" traditionally taught in marketing courses — product, price, promotion, place and people — are being disrupted by technology. These disruptions are causing the discipline of marketing to recede, and to be superseded by big data and martech, which connect brands via personal digital relationships, a.k.a., relationshipping.

Meanwhile, customer-centricity is displacing market-centricity. Unlike the prior state of goods and services, which were spread all around various physical marketplaces (or more recently across websites), our 21ˢᵗ century technology connects consumers with brands, placing all the information about products and services in the palms of their hands.

Today's Internet-based connectivity and customer-centricity now allows us to replace marketing with relationshipping, and gives us the consumerplace, versus the marketplace.

Before we explore the shift towards relationshipping, let's first discuss the ways that technology and brand personalization are dismantling the Five Ps of marketing:

P FOR PRODUCT

Historically, brands have studied their consumers to understand what to make, or what services to offer. Using manufactured products as the example, the resulting goods then moved from factory to distributor to market or store. This process is now being disrupted by the advent of product personalization.

For example, it has been more than eight years since I have set foot in a men's shoe store. Sneakers have become acceptable office attire for ad execs, so it's not surprising that over the years, I have developed loyalty to several brands — including Nike ID. To get a new personalized pair of sneakers, one visits the Nike website, goes to the ID models and customizes the selected sneaker model by selecting the size, color of sole, tongue, leather elements, cloth/fabric elements, laces and so forth, finally adding one's initials (which can go on the tongue or heel). Your customized, personalized sneakers are then delivered to your home in a matter of weeks. The prices are competitive with standard, non-personalized models.

Meanwhile, a New York retailer called My.Suit has stores that offer made-to-measure men's suits personalized via Internet technology. Once you become a customer and My.Suit has your measurements, you can use your online account to customize and personalize every detail of your suit via an experience they call Suit Builder: Pick a fabric, lining, number of front buttons, sleeve buttons, vents, pockets — then have your initials embroidered on the inside vest pocket or underneath the collar. Click to buy, and UPS drops off your customized, personalized, made-to-measure suit at your home in about two weeks. The prices of these suits are often less expensive than off-the-rack store brand suits.

Meanwhile, My.Suit understands the value of personal interaction with the product, so they offer a dual model; if you like, you can go to the store to touch and feel fabrics, and make the choices there with your consultant. Informed by your preferences, the consultant then enters it all into your account, and clicks to purchase. Two weeks later, your suit is delivered.

Thanks to the Internet and advancing technology, product (P) is moving aggressively toward product personalization.

P FOR PRICE

There are more than 20 price apps available for mobile smartphones. In the store, you scan the UPC (universal product code) code, stipulate a GPS radius, and the app gives the price of this product in all locations within that radius. Plus, you also get to compare what online sellers offer, in case you'd rather "showroom" what you are shopping for and order online.

One of my favorites of these pricing apps is Vivino. This app for oenophiles allows you snap a photo of any wine bottle label, and provides not only ratings of that wine, but also its average price in your designated area. You can also buy many wines directly from the app, and opt into Vivino emails with wine offers.

With price app technology in place, it is becoming increasingly difficult to overprice a product. Hence, the traditional "P for Price" is finding itself disrupted by technology and connectivity.

P FOR PERSON

This is the newest of the traditional marketing Five Ps and surfaced with the advent of the computerized prospect and customer databases some 50 years ago. (Before that, marketing had only the Four Ps.) Of course, people have always been part of the equation, but the emergence of computers in the late 1950s created the tool needed to put people into the targeting and personalization equation.

Several manufacturers produced mainframe computers from the late 1950s through the 1970s. The stateside group of manufacturers was colloquially known as "IBM and the Seven Dwarves" — usually Burroughs, UNIVAC, NCR, Control Data, Honeywell, General Electric and RCA, although lists vary. The use of computerized databases to conduct direct mail campaigns came about in the '60s, after IBM introduced the 360 mainframes.

The introduction of the IBM System/360 on April 7, 1964, heralded the arrival of a new family of computers that reshaped not only IBM, but also the entire computer industry. Direct mail address labels went from manual production to computerized systems. Things really got rolling with the upgrade to the S/370, which coincided with the first computerized census, the 1970 U.S. Census. The era of "overlaying" data on a list for better targeting was inaugurated. If the late '60s represented the birth of prospect and customer databases, then the '70s offered their adolescence — with target demographic profiles that fit the brand's model customer.

Before this time, mail communications had involved customer lists in manual formats, requiring mechanical systems to get the mailings out. With these new, more powerful computers, mail could at least be addressed in an automated way. From there, direct mail communications graduated to being personalized.

With the Internet came email. Though the first email was sent in 1971, the first commercialized systems for mass email emerged in the early 1990s. What had until that point been offline, quickly moved online. Today, brands can send personalized emails to customers and prospects alike.

For example, if you're an Amazon Prime member, you're well aware that Amazon knows who you are, what you buy and how to keep you fully up to date with new offers in your areas of interest — as well as reminders to repurchase via daily emails. With the Echo smart speaker and voice assistance from Alexa, you can talk directly to Amazon in order to get information and purchase.

Forgive me, but I can't resist relating one of my first Echo/Alexa experiences. Being an early adopter, I bought one of the first-generation Echo smart speakers (and paid $370 for it!). My second mistake was putting it in the kitchen, where my wife Donna — a fabulous cook — was in the process of hunting down a recipe for moussaka. I turned to the Echo and crowed, "Alexa, what is the recipe for moussaka?" Alexa immediately launched into a recitation of the ingredients, then into detailed steps to make the dish. Donna held up one hand, signaling her to stop. "George," she sighed, "We only need one bitch in the kitchen!"

Having been banished from our kitchen, the Echo and Alexa now reside in my office. I ask her about the weather.

Given the new technology — with the cloud, with big data, with single customer view and the customer data platform (pulled together from all the disparate databases around the enterprise) — we now have an identity that the brand wants to serve. The brand's *raison d'être* is to create a relationship with that personal identity, making every effort via email, mobile sites, texting and apps to build a rich customer lifetime value with it.

"P for Person" is moving from the unconnected world to being Internet-connected and relationship-managed by data-driven brand personalization.

P FOR PROMOTION

Illustrating the dramatic disruption of promotion is an impressive prediction: In five years, 75% of all U.S. marketing spend will go to three digital platforms — Google (largely comprised of paid search and YouTube); Facebook (which also houses Instagram and WhatsApp); and Amazon. Meanwhile, 2018 marked the first year that digital marketing communication spend surpassed TV ad spend in the US.

Before the Internet and digital media, marketers painted a bull's eye on the prospect and fired messages at them through (offline) media. The idea was to build such demand for the brand that the prospect's hand would move mere inches from the competitor's product to our advertised brand's product. This still happens, of course, as brand awareness will always be an important part of any complete strategy. But the Internet created a whole new world of brand engagement that flipped the unconnected, offline model completely around. That is to say, the Internet put the marketplace in the customer's hand, thus fostering a connected, customer-centric business model for the movement of goods and services.

Google took what had been the Yellow Pages and made it on-demand and interactive, all in the palm of your hand. Instead of it all beginning with the consumer being a target to be hit with an ad, it now all begins with the consumer initiating the customer journey by putting a search word into the search bar, or just visiting a brand site. Therefore, much of the battle for the consumer today begins with Google's ZMOT. Moving goods and services often begins with the consumer wanting something, and plugging search terms into the search bar. It behooves us, then, to move away from just "marketing" and to move toward an aggressively customer-centric approach that recognizes that the consumer is both connected and in charge, and that the brand's job is meet them where they are — creating the bond that delivers a strong relationship and rich customer lifetime value.

That's why it remains fundamentally important to have a strong search strategy and budget in place to compete. Because winning customers begins with the attempt to capture and bond with them at the customer-initiated outset, this discipline isn't "marketing"; it's relationshipping. Let's approach moving goods and services from a customer-centric perspective, rather than beginning with the product in a market (or on a website) and trying to sell, then send customers to wherever products sit.

With the consumer now in charge, promotion has been adjusting from awareness and selling in ads, to telling the brand story in all the places customers seek information. For that reason, creative — ads, if you will — is now joined with (and in some cases, surpassed by) work we call content. Why?

Imagine that the initial communication serves as a doorway to the brand's house. But this doorway exists in an environment of exploration and bonding, not yet buying and selling. What we see in the customer journey is that the Internet permits much more browsing and research than in days of yore. In fact, before digital connectivity, research was at best limited, or at worst impossible, with products physically and geographically scattered across markets.

So, relationshipping is different from marketing and selling that use advertising. Advertising has long used creative that is strategically designed to not only create awareness and image, but also to sell. What we see today with the gravitas of social media is content that the brand offers. That content joins the conversation in product discussion and ratings spaces, tells the brand story, conveys brand purpose and strategically approaches the consumer with the objective of building a relationship.

In this digitally connected world and construct, content is rapidly growing because of the new role of brand communications in the journey. As more of the journey begins with search and interaction in social spaces, content continues to grow and advertising gradually recedes.

General offline advertising will never disappear, of course. New media tend to reposition older media, not kill them. Reach will remain important to create awareness and support the digital engagement channels, but a new balance and order will be established. This balance will be more determined by and weighted towards content as we cultivate relationshipping to coexist with — and eventually surpass — marketing.

In addition to this change, direct-to-consumer (DTC) brands are helping to shift the shopping process by having the consumer explore merchandise at home, versus in a store. A good example: Warby Parker. If you have a current eye exam on record, this upscale eyewear boutique allows you to select five frames online to be mailed to your home. You try them all on, choose the one you want and, having made your selection, send all the samples back. In a week or so, your new prescription eyeglasses are delivered. This novel approach requires and defines relationshipping, versus marketing. Warby Parker achieves balance in this model by maintaining retail locations to provide the showroom element of the customer journey.

Promotion disruption has produced extremes, from a six-second bumper ad on YouTube (the door to the brand's house) to a three-minute tutorial video on the brand website (well within in the brand's house). Because this information is to be of service to the consumer, these brand videos can be safely described as content — effectively removing the stigma that the enterprise at hand is advertising, which is always selling. Content fosters a conversation and relationship with the brand, which of course can lead to a sale, however indirectly. However, the stigma of selling is softened.

One data point that supports the communications shift in promotion: 2018 became the first year in which digital ad spend surpassed TV ad spend in the U.S. This shift in spend will likely continue in the coming years as relationshipping advances, as more attention turns toward smartphones, tablets and other mobile devices, and as more shopping begins with search and connecting with brands on those digital devices.

The beginning of relationshipping is centered in digital data management platforms (DMPs) that hold individuals' digital online behavior in the search for and engagement with products and services. This allows the brand to deliver near-personalized digital engagement communications from which — with the first response — the relationshipping journey begins. The Internet has allowed the consumer multiple devices and touchpoints across which to meet and engage with the brand, and has given the brand a depth of storytelling, service and personalization never before possible. Promotion, which traditionally trafficked only in one direction, is now a two-way street.

P FOR PLACE

Perhaps the most dramatic disruption of any of the Ps is the one led by Amazon: distribution. We can think of Amazon as the best, most powerful example of e-tailing. (For excellent reading on the topic, I recommend *The Everything Store: Jeff Bezos and the Age of Amazon* by Brad Stone.) The Internet — in tandem with the USPS, UPS, FedEx and all the other delivery brands that come to your home or business — have powerfully disrupted distribution.

Instead of sending our factory-produced item to a distributor, so that it may then find its way into stores where people can buy and take it home, we now have a direct online purchase that the brand has made available in that channel. When purchased, it gets delivered to the consumer's mailbox or front porch, or perhaps dropped by drone in the back yard.

This shift is profound because e-tailing is more efficient than a retail distribution system, and is doing considerable damage to retailers and the value of real estate supporting that system. E-tailed goods are about to hit 20% of all goods purchased. If my retail store only has a 15% profit margin, and e-tailing takes away 20% of my sales, I'm underwater. It's only logical, then, that shopping malls are in the news as their anchor stores fail, and that mall offerings need to be changed if they are to survive.

This disruption is taking us to a mixed model: Traditional retailers like Target are adding direct-to-consumer digital options while direct-to-consumer brands like Bonobos, Warby Parker, Everlane, Casper and Allbirds are adding stores. (In fact, more than 20 have done so, and more are still to come.)

Those retail businesses that cannot adapt to the new disruption model face shrinking at best, and closing at worst. (Think of Macy's, which has closed hundreds of stores to adjust; Sears, which is hanging by a thread; Barney's, which has declared bankruptcy and is closing stores; or Payless Shoes, which has failed and is gone altogether.) Brands losing retail distribution have no choice but to figure out how to adjust to the new distribution model if they wish to survive.

With the customer now firmly in charge, the new brand focus lies in customer-centricity, brand personalization and relationshipping — the art and science of bonding the consumer to the brand digitally with final metric focus on generating optimum customer lifetime value.

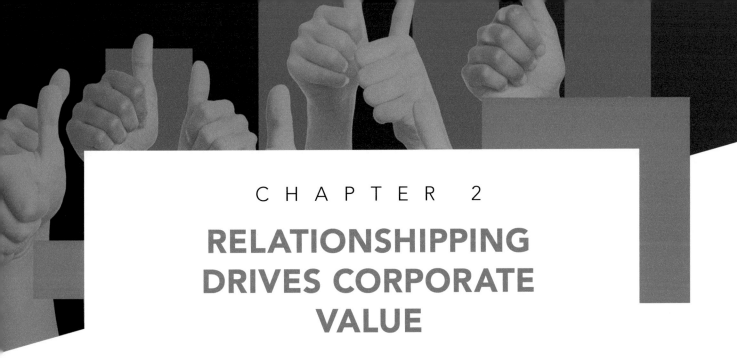

CHAPTER 2

RELATIONSHIPPING DRIVES CORPORATE VALUE

Connectivity and big data are changing how the C-suite needs to look at corporate valuation. Naturally, it makes sense that the value of your company depends on people buying your products and services. It also makes sense that a stronger and more strategic bond with customers makes for greater company value. But before this age of micro-moment digital connectivity and the resulting big data flows, there were no solid, reliable, current measures of the customer/brand relationship that allowed for accurate, up-to-date customer valuation, much less for rolling up those customer valuations into an estimate of the overall valuation of a company.

Today, we have taken the first steps in this direction. A small group of prescient financial analysts have been developing algorithms that rely on publicly disclosed *customer* metrics, which do a better job of predicting corporate value than do historical financial measures on their own.

This requires a change in perspective by the C-suite and by private equity and frankly all investment businesses putting capital in enterprises: the budgets directed to bonding customers to the enterprise must now be managed while understanding their impact on corporate value. Fair notice to C-titles: My charge is to spend the rest of my career advocating for an approach to running companies that connects the dots between corporate value and relationshipping.

At the 2018 DRUM Fast Track Summit in Atlanta, Dan McCarthy, Assistant Professor of Marketing at Emory University's Goizueta School of Business, introduced attendees to his work on customer-based corporate valuation (CBCV).

Dan is a member of a pioneering group of quantitative modelers using customer metrics to develop enterprise valuation algorithms that go beyond the standard discounted cash flow (DCF) valuation methods. He joined three other accomplished executives in this field to form Theta Equity Partners. The enterprise now serves some 25 clients in the financial services sector (think private equity, hedge fund and venture capital firms), as well as public companies and consulting firms.

One of the early analyses that brought a lot of interest in Theta was a study by two of their co-founders on Wayfair, Inc. (NYSE:W). At the time, their work implied that the stock was overvalued. This conclusion was waved off by some within the investment community, but there were a couple of funds following the work that shorted the stock. When the next earnings period revealed the softness that Theta predicted, the stock went down. Not only did the short funds do well, the event also helped put Dan and Theta on the map.*

One of the advantages of CBCV is that the method of customer lifetime value metrics in the algorithms so far has proven to yield more accurate cash flow predictions than DCF. One of Theta's offerings is a multi-year forecast of overall future revenues driven by CLV metrics.

Remember: There are three main components of relationshipping execution. We have covered the first — that is, the art and science of relationshipping — as well as the second, the connection between customer data and deriving better corporate valuation calculation and prediction. The third component, however, involves implementing the practice inside the enterprise, or putting relationshipping into play. For now, though, let's explore the ways that the emergence of big data and insights has recalibrated the development of successful brand, product and relationshipping strategy.

*There are excellent illustrative cases on the Theta Equity Partners website, www.thetaequity.com. In addition, Dan McCarthy and Peter Fader published an excellent article in the January-February 2020 issue of *Harvard Business Review*, which can be found at https://hbr.org/2020/01/the-loyalty-economy#how-to-value-a-company-by-analyzing-its-customers. The article clearly explains the techniques using customer data to improve the prediction of corporate valuation.

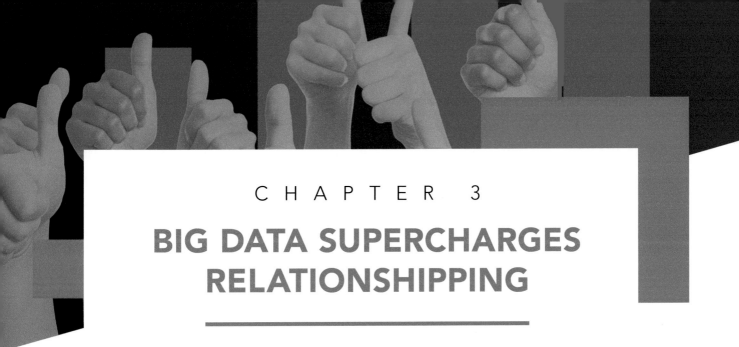

CHAPTER 3
BIG DATA SUPERCHARGES RELATIONSHIPPING

Given that relationshipping drives enterprise value, how does the C-suite build the customer base and improve customer lifetime value (CLV)? Developing an answer to this question should be a top priority for any CEO. I strongly recommend that the enterprise have at least two elements in place to solve the equation: a customer data platform (CDP) filled with big data to drive analytics, and a high-powered, up-to-date, analytics-powered research tool.

There are a number of basic tasks the enterprise needs to perform in order to put that foundation in place. First, it's vital to address the fact that customer data is scattered all around the enterprise in subsets. So, Task Number One is to pull all that big data together into a CDP, unduplicated for each person, prospect or customer.

Task Number Two involves putting analytics resources in place, whether in house or via an external partner. This step begins furnishing input and insights from customer behavior to feed the strategies and tactics for building CLV. Here are some of the basic questions that the CDP and analytics may address:*

1. **Market mix optimization.** Where should I spend the extra dollar? What is the optimal marketing mix? What is the relationshipping return on investment (RROI) for each media spend, based on contribution to the final metric, CLV?
2. **Price elasticity and demand.** By how much will sales drop if we increase price by 5%? What should be our price range across products, geography and segment?
3. **Multi-touch attribution.** Which digital channels are most effective to drive traffic and conversions? How do channels interact? What is the best path to conversion on the website? Tied to CLV?
4. **Market basket analysis.** What products are often purchased together? How will customers respond to bundling of different products?

5. **Propensity to engage and purchase.** Which customers are most likely to purchase in the future? What are the elements that contribute to moving from x to y? Recommendations of next best offer? How do we cross-sell/upsell to likely customers?

6. **Customer segmentation.** What customer groups are most meaningful to my business? How can demographic, behavioral and psychographic information influence customers?

7. **Customer attrition.** Which customers are most likely to attrite, and why? What actions should we take to retain profitable customers?

8. **High-value/lower-funnel activities.** What activities on the website are most consequential to purchase? How can relationshipping drive lower-funnel activities to increase conversion? What should my KPIs be in order to feed, then optimize RROI (i.e., relationshipping return on investment)?

Bottom line: A well-constructed and maintained CDP allows for robust analysis to get at the heart of what's going on with customers and prospects. Those insights in turn can be used to build the customer base, CLV and the business.

Task Number Three involves implementing some serious research horsepower, and focusing on what is most important: what will cause a person to switch to your brand.

One of my earliest lessons in relationshipping was imparted to me by Shirley Young, director of research at Grey Advertising when I joined in 1980. Shirley emphasized that whatever product or service you are bringing to the consumer, they already have something competitive in place — in reality as well as in their minds. So, the first engagement and first sale require the person to make a switch from what is already in place.

This situation calls for an essential insight: What will create the highest propensity for the consumer to switch from what they have and instead engage your brand in that space? Your C-suite needs a high-powered research tool that can find those elements of your offering to generate the highest odds for a switch.

There are many high-quality research offerings out there to do just this. At DRUM Agency, for instance, we use LaunchPad.™ The LaunchPad tool is configured to focus on the odds of switching, helping the C-suite understand what is most important about the product and engagement. It measures what combination of elements has the highest impact on the propensity to cause a prospect to switch. By combining traditional research techniques — for example, discrete choice model research — with the availability of custom online panel configuration, then having the research results analyzed in a high-powered simulation model, LaunchPad has proven to:

- Pretest a number of important product attribute, communication and offer variables to identify the ones that will advance the business.
- Yield the right relationshipping approach to each persona or segment by geographies.
- Cut time from test to fielding winning communications in market, which not only increases share of market and sales but also saves money by eliminating testing waste.

Because LaunchPad has consistently produced double-digit gains in engagement, nearly all DRUM Agency clients have used it to keep winning elements in play.

LaunchPad improves upon the traditional "test, read and implement" process. This outmoded process can take months, can be hit-or-miss, and is expensive — especially if none of the tested variables work. Traditionally, the process goes something like this:

1. Brainstorm concepts.
2. Determine best concepts/elements to test and create the test matrix.
3. Implement operational requirements for in-market, live testing.
4. Select prospect audience, finalize creative, produce landing page, email, mail and ads.
5. Execute test campaign, track response.
6. Measure results, determine viability against control, maintain back-end support through transition, decide on rollout.

One of the key failings we discovered in this old approach to research and testing is that a positive research finding alone is often not enough to move the needle. A simple example: finding that blue beats red in the research, then going with blue versus red in the live, in-market test … only to find it did not move the needle, and did not get better results.

LaunchPad can be used to explore new product attributes, claims, offers, labeling, messages and images. Using elements in existing control communications, it can also level-set tests against established in-market offers and product features. It has revealed to us by way of the analytics simulator that gains — i.e., moving the needle — in test results over control results depend on the best combination of a number of key factors yielding the highest odds for a switch.

Its power is most palpable when the research findings are put into its simulator to calculate odds on all the various combinations of researched elements. In other words, the horsepower of analytics is being combined with the sophistication of a discrete-choice online survey to supercharge results. To illustrate, one study LaunchPad tested:

- Forced choice among 18 product sets
- 18 product sets presented for 72 offers

- Patterns of choice demonstrated
- 612,360,000 possible combinations analyzed
- 29 billion possible outcomes tested

When all this is calculated, only one set of combined elements (such as product attributes, offer elements, language, competitor, geography) wins in the simulator over the others. Upon testing, the winning set of elements has consistently beat control communications — raising response usually by double digits.

The simulator allows the marketer to test the market potential of various product features, labeling, offers and message combinations against specific consumer segments in competition with specific brands in their area. It also gives the team, especially product management and communications, the opportunity to understand what works in market prior to product rollout.

Unlike the traditional approach to testing described above, the tool allows for lower testing expenses (usually at least 50% less) and higher performing offers and/or efforts. Meanwhile, it encourages dynamic product development, actionable competitive intelligence and significantly less time to market.

The tool identifies the combinations of product attributes, offer elements and messaging that, against the specific geographic competitive brands, will drive the greatest intent to respond and switch — doing so quickly, cost-effectively and with statistical confidence. It performs with less test cost and with better results than traditional in-market testing methods. Meanwhile, results have been proven to work in every channel, improving performance in email, display, video, print, direct mail and telesales.

Let's look at an example from a study performed some time ago in the area of cable TV service for businesses. (Non-disclosure agreements prevent me from sharing the brand.) We began with the relative influence of attributes on intent to switch in a study offering service to businesses. Pricing dominated in terms of offer attributes, but that occurs often and is hardly differentiating. The next influential attribute, meanwhile, was speed. And although attributes like a gift with purchase, rewards program, desktop portal and static IP had no impact on likelihood to switch services (acquisition), it was possible that they could impact retention.

We were able to create success not only by featuring speed, but also by finding the right way to communicate it, the right way to compare to the competition, and the right way to ensure satisfaction with speed. It impresses me that today — more than a decade later — speed is still a winning element used to attract converts in this service area.

Because the LaunchPad simulator is interactive, the user can insert the combinations they wish to test. The simulator aids in finding the optimum combination of elements to use in the promotion and communications going out today. And product managers get to see what is most important and set priorities for product development.

For relationshipping to add maximum value to the enterprise, relationshipping strategy needs the foundation of insights from analytics — preferably from the CDP. Strategy is also enhanced by the high-powered findings from a research tool like LaunchPad. Relationshipping then relies on first using data-driven digital media to initiate a brand relationship, then unifying that digital outreach with all other media used across the journey.

Media never live in a vacuum; for best results, they should be unified and measured by a final metric — customer lifetime value — not just by the middle metric measure of a specific channel or touchpoint.

*Thanks to Jonathan Zajicek, DRUM Agency Chief Analytics Officer, for the list.

CHAPTER 4
DIGITAL MEDIA DELIVERS A CRUCIAL STARTING POINT

The use of media to create brand awareness and to convert prospects is an ancient strategy. However, martech and digital interaction have changed it considerably — in large part because connected audiences deposit a lot of information about themselves online as they search and shop each day. The big data they generate online now gives the brand data management platforms (DMPs), which guide the careful selection of media audiences whose online behavior models their likelihood to be customers.

Having spent much of my career immersed in direct marketing, I can't help but note that Internet, its data and its technology have turned most media into "direct media" — all measurable for engagement and conversion. Today, relationshipping begins in general digital media, in the consumerplace, via platforms that, minute by minute, individual by individual, are recording consumer demand.

Again, it's essential to pay attention to where the puck is going, not where it is now. Studies show that, in several years, the vast majority of all media spend will go to Amazon, Google and Facebook. Yes, TV is still powerful in its capacity to generate awareness — even if it is shifting shape, thanks to streaming and addressable options. And although digital spend recently surpassed TV spend in the U.S. for the first time, brands will absolutely continue use TV for awareness. After all, TV is a channel that can and will support relationshipping. Meanwhile, seemingly antiquated media like terrestrial radio, direct mail, even print remain highly relevant. Sales promotion still involves a healthy spend, along with social media and paid social media.

Sooner or later, however, we will come back to the fact that, in order to be successful, brand communications across the media spectrum must be unified. In doing so, we will resist eliminating *any* media spend that can be shown to build the brand relationships and the business effectively.

Relationshipping begins with near-personalized messages, using digital media at the individual level, with (almost) real-time demand data in DMPs to target the right audiences. *All* media — whether online or offline — must work together toward a common objective of growing customer lifetime value, consistently and affordably.

Relationshipping starts with an individual's online behavior, and sustains itself by reaching that prospect through media focused on measurable conversion. Prospects' identities reside in digital spaces, so brands can not only target relevant audiences, but also take the first steps toward relationships with personalized (and near-personalized) conversations. Those interactions often allow the prospect to raise their hands and opt into the brand relationship voluntarily. So, what once was possible with data-driven personalized direct mail, for example, has since been actualized in digital media. Given Internet connectivity and mobility, as well as the advent of DMPs, media spends will continue to migrate to these powerful new digital spaces where individuals can register their needs, often in real time.

Data management platforms unify brands by collecting, organizing and activating first-, second- and third-party audience data from any source — including online, offline, mobile and beyond. To make the brand data robust, most use data from a major external, big-brand DMP supplier. Popular DMP providers include:

- Adobe Audience Manager
- Salesforce DMP
- OnAudience.com
- Snowflake
- Oracle DMP
- SAS Data Management
- Mapp DMP
- Nielsen DMP
- Krux
- Lotame
- Turn
- CoreAudience
- Knotice

The DMP serves the backbone of data-driven marketing, allowing businesses to gain unique, actionable insights into their customers. A DMP allows your business to:

- Gather all your collected data in a single place.
- Use third-party data to uncover new markets.
- Gain audience insights through analytics.
- Create a holistic view of your customers.
- Target your audience by creating custom segments for your DSP.
- Comply with the GDPR and CCPA.

While a DMP is used to store and analyze data, a demand-side platform (DSP) acts as a programmatic buyer for digital advertising based on the consumer information offered by the DMP. That is, the information that the DMP collects is segmented and selected for your brand target, then transferred to its DSP, which in turn drives digital ad buying decisions. Top DSPs include:

- Facebook Ads Manager
- Rocket Fuel
- MediaMath
- Amazon (AAP)
- DoubleClick
- LiveRamp
- Choozle
- TubeMogul

My purpose here is not to trumpet the value of any big media company in particular, but rather to emphasize the fact that the brand and its C-suite need to put the DMP-to-DSP foundation in place with their media partners, if they haven't already done so. This foundation provides the capability to deliver programmatic media with algorithm-generated and -automated, custom-configured creative that aligns with the target audiences. Conversion goals are set, reviewed and adjusted — all in order to build the customer base, initiate relationshipping and add to CLV. Once the prospect forms the customer relationship by opting into the brand, relationshipping has occurred; it then sets the stage for subsequent relationshipping efforts like eCRM.

The journey from DMP to DSP, to programmatic and algorithm-generated relevant ads, is more than a core practice of digital media; it's the inaugural moment for relationshipping. However, for best return on ad spend (ROAS), this digital front-end now has to be unified with all media for optimized results.

UNIFYING MEDIA

It is ironic that the tremendous advance of digital media gives brands greater efficiency and effectiveness while simultaneously fracturing customer experience. After all, much offline creative takes place in a siloed context. In addition to digital media, we still have all the other effective offline efforts — such as TV, radio, print, direct mail and sales promotion materials. A cohesive, unified brand strategy involves pulling together all campaign touchpoint and communications elements into consistent brand relationshipping communications.

Most media firms have a director of integrated media — a discipline that focuses fundamentally on the results of all media placements. Analytics is now tying those together with a final measurement, such as cost per account, or better yet, CLV. (Remember: Evaluation exclusively through middle metrics like cost-per-click or per-visit can cost a brand millions).

Given that a big contributing factor to the fractured customer experience has been the siloing of the media function, it's essential to restore a holistic approach to media touchpoints. The effort toward unification relies on brand strategy and creative as key inputs. As we will address in the upcoming discussion of technology, along with media unification comes the task of unifying martech platforms. But strategic unification of media and communications comes first.

Relationshipping strategy involves a return to a discipline that existed before the trend toward disparate, siloed communication disciplines — with media in one company, direct in another, sales promotion in another, and so on. How can we begin to tie it all back together? We can start by uniting all the contributing disciplines with a single relationshipping strategy that answers these six questions:

1. What thoughts?
2. In whose minds?
3. In the face of what competition?
4. Supported by what analytics?
5. Delivered in what media?
6. With what linked technology?

We are only beginning to take down silo walls and to unify all communication efforts with a consistent, effective, journey-long customer brand experience. After 40+ years of specialization and siloing, our challenge in the C-suite is to put it back together. These six essential questions generate a strategy process document that should be reviewed and approved by at least six agency officers, as well as key brand stakeholders (particularly CMO and product management). The agency executives should include:

- Chief Strategy Officer
- Chief Creative Officer
- Account Director
- Media Director
- Chief Technology Officer
- Chief Analytics Officer

By answering six key questions and getting six sign-offs, we have a chance to unify all the media, developing a consistent customer experience of the brand for relationshipping media communications. An approved, interdisciplinary strategy document helps to generate creative and content that are unified across the journey. All touchpoint communications should focus on optimizing CLV, which often demands that they work together in serving the customer consistently.

CHAPTER 5

RELATIONSHIPPING TELLS THE BRAND STORY WITH CONTENT

In the days before the Internet, before YouTube, before display and before social media, "creative" referred to ads in offline media. Its ideal form remains the 30-second brand spot. Its Valhalla? The Super Bowl.

Branding and the creation of brand standards have always been an industry in their own right. What is the logo? What is the tagline? Is there a mascot? Those considerations led to rules for a brand's application to print, collateral materials, direct mail, sales promotion, store signage, radio spots and so forth.

Meanwhile, creative needed to be guided by advertising strategy that answered essential questions: *What thoughts do we want to place, and into whose mind? In the face of what competition? With what call to action?* Remember that this approach involved painting media bulls-eyes on the brand targets and firing ads at them — all within the unconnected marketplace. In this system, the emphasis would lie on the FMOT (First Moment of Truth), so that the prospect's hand would move 12 inches away from competitor toward our brand, eventually making the purchase.

Then came the Internet and connectivity, taking the arrow that pointed from brand to consumer and reversing it. For the first time, the consumer sought out specific products or services, and was truly in charge.

This changes the emphasis from the FMOT to ZMOT (Zero Moment of Truth). Google coined the term "micro-moment" to describe the entry of words into the search bar, effectively capturing the notion that demand is live, 24/7. The click that starts the search process represents the ZMOT. At this point, it's no longer about our prospect's hand moving 12 inches in a store aisle; it's about whether our brand and links pop to the top of the search engine results page. Should the next click bring the shopper to our site, the creative challenge no longer pertains to ads; it's all about content. How is the brand represented there on the site and in all online spaces? How does the brand speak in order to engage the prospect and initiate a relationship?

The ZMOT also determines whether or not our brand joins the conversation to tell our story, offering advice and assistance to the prospective customer when they visit all branded social spaces as part of their research before buying. Consumers trust brand advocates and reviews more than they trust advertising. This is why brand content is so important — and why influencer initiatives are growing.

Search, site visits and social spaces have given birth to content. As content grows in contact with the consumer, creative declines. In addition to excellent brand creative, then, it is vital that a brand have excellent content and execution.

ENGAGEMENT STRATEGY

My charge to the C-suite is to put in place at your enterprise a new strategy discipline that unites outbound, media-delivered creative with the consumer-sought content. The goal is consistent branding and a consistent brand experience. As this goal is executed on a granular basis using the latest data, analytics and technology skills, it will lead to brand personalization.

Creative and content efforts should not begin without all C-level stakeholders and executional managers signing off on strategy. An approval document should look something like this:

Brand Creative and Content Communications Strategy

1. *What message?*
2. *Do we want what customer to receive?*
3. *In the face of what competition?*
4. *Supported by what analytics? (I.e., Where are they online? What keywords do they use? Is our site harvesting?)*
5. *Delivered by what media or platforms, across what calendar?*
6. *Supported by what linked technology platforms?*
7. *Using what brand image, positioning, engagement invitations, offers and calls to action?*

CONTENT MARKETING

Who better to answer the question of how to define content marketing than the Content Marketing Institute itself? By their estimation, content marketing is:

> …[a] strategic marketing approach focused on creating and distributing valuable, relevant and consistent content to attract and retain a clearly-defined audience — and, ultimately, to drive profitable customer action.
>
> Content marketing is important, not just because it works for building trust, generating leads and cultivating customer loyalty, but because it has become the new normal from the consumer side. It is, in itself, helping to evolve what customers expect from the brands they interact with.
>
> Content marketing helps to improve conversions because it allows you to connect with and educate your leads and customers. Not only are you working to build trust and relationships, but you are also encouraging conversions by giving consumers the information they need to make an educated purchasing decision.

The most common relationshipping objectives involve lead generation, brand awareness and thought leadership. In content relationshipping, a core practice is to clearly define audiences (or even individuals), measuring content engagement against those objectives with precision. We want to know how the spend and/or budget contributes to CLV — or another final metric, such as cost per account.

Content begins on the brand website. There, the brand purpose and brand story are laid out, with centralized customer information and service. One of the top content forms on websites is the educational video, usually 90 to 180 seconds in length. This content augments any other digital art and copy on the site, as well as to any downloadable PDFs, blog entries or other material.

If relationshipping communications strategy sets the tone on the site, content relationshipping can then expand to the creation and sharing of material (e.g., videos, blogs, conversation posts, infographics, case studies, eBooks, white papers and many other forms) in all the other appropriate online spaces.

Brent Kuhn, advertising veteran and founder of BKV (now part of DRUM Agency), contributes the following approach to winning creative execution of content:

> It is important to understand that, to get the most out of content relationshipping, products and services can generally be dropped into one of two buckets: One, products that are brand image-driven, where the advertising is not necessarily

looking for an immediate response, but rather to educate, make aware and develop positive attitudes. And two, products that seek to generate some type of action now — such as an immediate sale or a lead. According to a 2016 Comscore study, 80% of online advertising content is seeking some sort of a response now. Thus, most of the online content you do will fall into Bucket #2.

Kuhn notes that an all-time great brand agency Benton & Bowles took the position that if your advertising doesn't sell, it isn't really creative. That's why it's essential to remember that, whatever your product or service, your content will be competing in the same media as your competitors. Therefore, any content you create must be compelling.

He also emphasizes a few fundamental rules to which relationshippers must adhere in order to maximize content effectiveness and to outpace competitors:

- Speak in terms of "you" – not "I."
- Sell benefits, features support.
- Speak as a person, not as a corporation.
- Keep words, sentences and paragraphs short.
- Lead with a major benefit.
- Don't just say it. Prove it!
- Your offer should be clear. If a person has to try and figure it out, you have lost him or her.
- Specifics sell; generalities don't.
- No one needs a solution without a problem.
- A large percentage of buying choices are made on emotion or impulse.

Brand content not only promotes the brand, but also is intended to engage, help and serve the exploring consumer, as well as existing customers.

It is highly likely that your brand content — no matter how well-crafted or effective — will appear in many places, over a breadth of online platforms. This has contributed to an inconsistent customer experience and suboptimal CLV. Mending that fracture, and in turn increasing CLV, requires an integrated tech stack, a topic we'll explore in the next chapter.

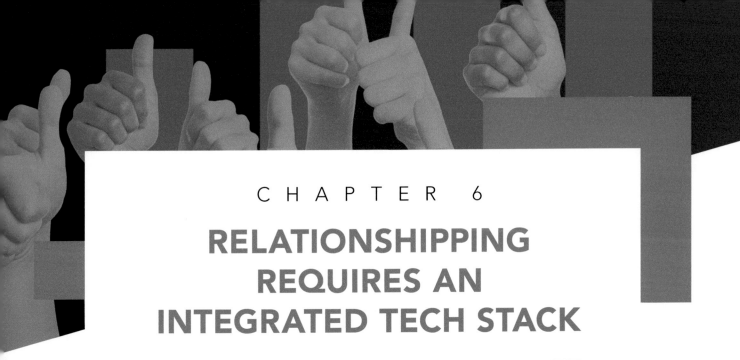

RELATIONSHIPPING REQUIRES AN INTEGRATED TECH STACK

At this writing, there are more than 7,000 martech platforms available. Given that your firm may use more than one platform internally, and given that any relationshipping firms you may engage have their own platforms, there is now an imperative need to stitch them all together.

Specifically, there may be many databases sprinkled throughout your enterprise, as well as throughout the outside firms you work with. In addition to marketing databases, it's not uncommon for there to be brand website database(s), a sales database, a customer services database, as well as others.

Your analytics team — or an outside analytics partner — needs to be empowered to pull all those database records together in order to create the single customer view (SCV), or in more recent parlance, "identity." In other words, it's essential to maintain a single, authoritative, database (and data-based) view of your prospects and customers. In pursuing that goal, your IT director and any outside partner enlisted to assist the mission can create the log of all platforms used by the brand that impact relationshipping. From that point on, the task involves putting in place the systems and procedures to allow all platforms to work together.

From a technological standpoint, there is much to be said about the implementation of these goals. Predictably, that discussion is highly complex and requires greater technical detail than can be addressed sufficiently in this volume. For the purposes of relationshipping, then, it should suffice simply to identify the importance of the space and the need for a fully integrated tech stack.

CHAPTER 7
BRAND PERSONALIZATION IS HERE

Just today, I downloaded a report on the tipping point for, and fast arrival of, Internet of Things (IoT) coming in 2020. Examples of such connected "things": We can now talk to our cars, our refrigerators and our home security systems. Likewise, the presence of automated assistants like Siri and Alexa in our homes connects us to the outside world like never before.

One quick anecdote: During one particularly botched exchange with Siri, I lamented to my wife Donna, "Siri doesn't understand me!" Donna replied, "Why should she be different than any other woman?"

Robots are catching on.

Only recently, it was announced that BMW and Audi will involve Alexa next year, providing automated assistance both to the driver and to the vehicle. We can expect much more of this type of movement toward AI-enabled devices and the IoT.

So, the C-suite must ask the question: Do our customers want to talk to the brand? Is that conversation key to our movement towards brand personalization? It is vital to focus on personalization platforms and software in the enterprise, unifying the disparate data from points of prospect and customer contact in order to have a good relationship. To me, that's the very essence of relationshipping: keeping good data on interactions, and using it to customize and personalize. Today, advancing CLV relies on insights from this customer data and the ability to deliver "what's in it for me" to prospects and customers.

Another source of impact on the growth of AI and intelligent devices will be big data growing even bigger. This data explosion is likely to put another task on the schedules of the C-suite — the chief technology officer and head of analytics, in particular — to determine how best to incorporate this data set into prospect and customer identity. The customer data platform (CDP) becomes even more important to maintain, nurture and keep up to speed.

Management, platform, software and systems are all essential to brand personalization. However, no discussion of customer data is complete without mentioning privacy. Approval, control and security involving company use of customer data are top priorities. In Europe, there is the General Data Protection Regulation (GDPR); subsequently many states are exploring and passing privacy legislation — above all, California with its CCPA (California Consumer Privacy Act). The GDPR sets out seven key principles:

1. Lawfulness, fairness and transparency
2. Purpose limitation
3. Data minimization
4. Accuracy
5. Storage limitation
6. Integrity and confidentiality (security)
7. Accountability

According to the law, these seven principles should undergird any organization's approach to processing personal data.

Reinforcing this approach to privacy and relationshipping are findings from a survey eMarketer conducted in late 2018.

 The top finding was that 69% of internet users are comfortable sharing personal information when it is clear to them how the enterprise will use it. They want the brand to promise not to share it or sell it to other entities (66%). If the brand gives the consumer some kind of compensation then again 66% are OK with sharing their data. The comfort zone is only 59% when they have not been a victim of any breach, leak or fraudulent use of their data so far in their internet experience. This suggests that people are wary of hacking, and reinforces the need to make a clear promise in Relationshipping to protect the consumer's information, giving them assurance as indicated below.

So, when a prospective customer visits your site to engage, she is first confronted with a legal privacy policy to "accept" (which corporate counsel will insist upon). Beyond that, though, relationshipping encourages us to begin the conversation by offering a promise to prospects that would have a relationship with our brand. In plain English: *"If you allow us to use your personal interactions with our brand to serve you better, we promise to give you control of your data on our platforms, never to share this data with outside entities without your permission and to deploy the highest data security measures possible to prevent hacking."*

In 1999-2000, when I served as chairman of the Direct Marketing Association (which has since been absorbed by the Association of National Advertisers), privacy was a top priority. People's fear of harm from their data being used improperly almost always exceeds the actual harm. Audiences rarely understand how data is used to make their navigation of products and services relevant and efficient.

One example involves setting up the Do Not Mail list some years ago at the Direct Marketing Association. As members, every major corporation contributed their customer mailing addresses, so that a questionnaire could be sent and returned by consumers, forming the Do Not Mail database. On this questionnaire, the first question allowed consumers to opt out from all third-class (i.e., advertising) mail. It was then followed by category-specific questions allowing opt-in to areas of interest — women's fashion, men's fashion, home goods and so forth. Only 11% of the 120,000,000+ homes that received this questionnaire opted out of third-class mail. All others volunteered to receive advertising mail for items and services they were interested in.

To date, there has not been an equivalent exercise in the digital spaces; all brands are on their own. It would be useful to educate consumers about the ways data helps them shop, but to my knowledge, there is no organized industry effort on that front.

Another example: retargeting. If you go on Google and search for a sneaker, your device's cookie data is available. Later, when you visit a weather forecast website, the digital display ad on that screen features a sneaker brand. There generally are two reactions to the practice of retargeting: 1) "Sneakers are now following me around! My privacy has been invaded, and it's creepy." 2) "Oh, wow. I really like that sneaker! … [CLICK.]"

Personally, I'd rather see an ad for a sneaker than an ad for a brassiere.

Today, the digital ad industry is facing a post-cookie, first-party data world. Keep in mind that targeted advertising has always existed, attempting to make the ad spend relevant, efficient and effective. Audiences have long accepted traditional ad-supported media, and more or less consciously understand that the low (or free) subscription cost of that media comes from advertisers paying to get it front of you. We are all equally used to ignoring — even skipping — ads that don't interest us in offline media.

Digital is new, different and, given mobile devices, far more personal. It strikes me that these are the very reasons — the newness and personal intimacy — that people have such visceral reactions to ads in these spaces, expressing anxiety about an invasion of privacy. Perhaps over time, they will get used to it.

At one point, Facebook contemplated a test that charged users a fee in exchange for an ad-free version. This practice in commercial digital spaces would have been educational, and would have had the effect of consumers opting into digital ads, rather than paying a subscription fee.

From the brand perspective, my recommendation remains full transparency, full control for the customer and full effort to ensure security of data.

The pace of change in our new martech world is breathtaking. It has changed how the brand is bonding with customers and serving them. It emphasizes the need for a robust and personally focused CDP for the enterprise. More important, though, it changes marketing into relationshipping.

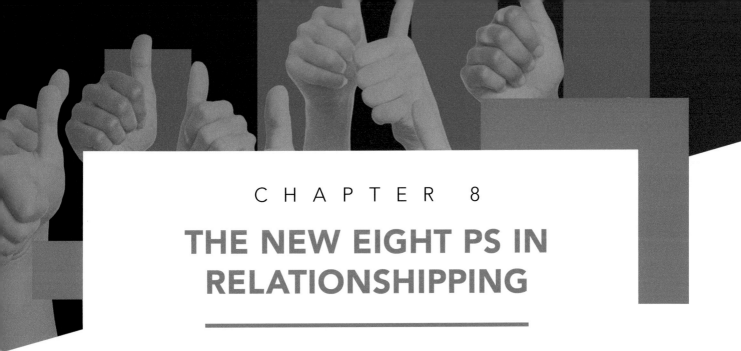

THE NEW EIGHT PS IN RELATIONSHIPPING

The "Five Ps" traditionally taught in marketing courses — product, price, promotion, place and people — are being disrupted by technology. Meet the new "Ps": Personalization, product personalization, presence, pervasiveness, publishing, platform, prediction and privacy.

With the introduction of smartphones about a decade ago, connecting billions of us with purveyors of goods and services around the globe has brought about a dramatic pace of change.

It's worth repeating: Consumers want to connect to brands. The connection begins with search, then centers in the brand website or app. This shift has not only put the consumer in charge; it has also fostered the consumer's desire for the brand to know them and to customize the product and service for them, if not completely personalize it.

In the words of the consumer: *Please know me. In my pressured micro-moment world, please interact with relevance and efficiency.* The bottom line for the C-suite: After product satisfaction, heading towards personalization is vital to staying competitive. This dynamic changes the traditional Five Ps of marketing into the new Eight Ps of relationshipping.

PERSONALIZATION

This first P can be a brief review, as we have already discussed the importance of the brand CDP — which needs to be organized for identity. CDP needs to keep up to date, accurate data of all interactions and transactions in order to generate insights for the purpose of analytics. Along with progress toward towards personalization, the CDP will support the AI necessary for an automated assistant to serve the customer knowledgeably and effectively.

At the Association of National Advertisers (ANA), more than 300 of the members voted "personalization" as the 2019 Marketing Word of the Year — beating out terms like "equality and inclusion," "data," and "in-house." Why? Because consumers now expect it, making brand personalization not only a major business trend, but also an essential capability. Below is a sampling of comments from voting members:

- *"Personalization is what customers expect. Every current and prospective customer expects that your brand knows them, and can deliver what they want."*
- *"Consumers are busy — too busy to invest time with anything that's not relevant to them personally. It's all about relevance, a.k.a. personalization: 'Make it all about me.'"*
- *"We now have the tools to pay off this benefit. Technology is enabling marketers to personalize consumer experiences and communication."*
- *"In today's world of 'me,' personalization is how people want to consume information. Experiences need to be relevant and unique to the end user at nearly every interaction."*
- *"We're all striving to show value to customers in a way that's relevant to them. Technology is changing the way marketers are able to do so, and we're all united by our efforts to showcase personalization."*
- *"As marketers, we can no longer think about customers as just a single large group. If we assume all customers are the same, then we are not meeting their needs."*
- *"Personalization is the holy grail of brand marketing. It provides the ability to speak directly to the consumer or shopper with the right message, at the right time, in the right medium."*

According to the ANA's Marketing Knowledge Center "Ask the Expert" service, member questions on personalization started to pick up in 2018 and accelerated sharply in 2019. The team issued a report on personalization in mid-2019 that included these highlights:

- More than half of consumers expect companies to know their buying habits and anticipate their needs.
- Half of marketers plan to increase investments in personalization technology.
- One report participant identified personalization as the most important marketing trend of this century.

Despite the promise of personalization, marketers should use caution with their personalization strategies and tactics. Per the "Ask the Expert" report, data suggests that consumers can be underwhelmed by marketing efforts to personalize interactions; meanwhile, more personalization does not necessarily provide a better experience. In fact, there is some consumer skepticism, lack of understanding and even mistrust over the use of data for marketing purposes.

Nevertheless, personalization presents significant opportunities for marketers to deliver more relevant communications and experiences for consumers and customers alike.

PRODUCT PERSONALIZATION

This particular P is best managed by the product management team. To wit: Because I am a regular Levi's direct buyer, the company recently contacted me to introduce their Levi's Future Finish offering. Here is how the Levi's website describes how to customize the Custom 502 product:

- Laser technology allows you to customize the wash of these jeans
- Choose a pattern, level of distressing, overall tint and special back patch; our original back patch is made of leather, and fluorescent color options are made of FSC-certified Jacron paper
- This innovative process uses fewer chemicals for a cleaner jean with the same craftsmanship we're known for
- Fits with extra room for comfort
- Tapered through the leg for a modern look
- Made with sustainable, TENCEL™ fabric

Once these are ordered, all the information goes into the CDP and serves the "buy again" email, while also delivering insight into what the customer may be inclined to purchase next. (Amazon has been using collaborative filtering for 20 years to generate relevant offer suggestions for the next purchase.) Once the customer personalizes their product, the brand is enabled to focus on a more relevant exchange going forward.

PRESENCE AND PERVASIVENESS

In an age of "always on" and micro-moments (i.e., the ZMOT, when search patience provides the brand a few seconds to engage or lose out), it's vital that the brand be there for its potential audience. Specifically, the website needs to be current and fully functional, including landing pages and microsites that are used to engage. The brand also needs to be alive and up to date in all the social spaces: Facebook, Instagram, Pinterest and YouTube, plus all relevant places for the brand's vertical, as well all the blogs that influencers and interested shoppers might use and visit.

Brands can no longer sleep. At any time of the day when the consumer shows up, the brand needs to be present, and ready to engage.

PUBLISHING

These days, it is vital to tell the brand story, along with the brand being of service. Brand purpose has become vital to all stakeholders. In particular, Millennial and Generation Z consumers want their workplace to give them career purpose. It should come as no surprise, then, that they would gravitate to brands whose purpose aligns explicitly with their values. So, in addition to advertising, brands must move toward becoming publishers of their own brand story, emphasizing the brand purpose. White papers and robust blog content amplify the brand by giving their consumers the most enrichment possible.

The gravity of this gesture sometimes escapes attention at the C-suite level. Consumers take brands into their lives. Consumers want to talk to others about the brand. They want to feel good enough about the brand to welcome its logo into their lives and to wear it as a badge of pride. And in a relationship, the consumer wants to be favored: *Can I get to the front of the line, and have deals please?* The value of the consumer relationship needs to be communicated clearly. Given our connected world and its efficiency to disseminate information, brands are now publishers.

PLATFORM

The brand platform online (or app) must provide an exceptional experience. Think Amazon — one of the best platforms to emulate.

PREDICTION

If your C-suite lacks an in-house analytics team to focus on all the prospect and customer metrics in the CDP, then it is vital to employ an outside partner firm for the task.

I describe omnichannel optimization as unified communications — the goal being to broaden the idea beyond just spending budgets, such that communications work well together creatively for a unified brand experience. For relationshipping to work well, it is important to have excellent analytic capabilities. Strong analytics drives the ability to predict where the brand is going for prospects and customers.

This is vital now because corporate valuation is moving from discounted cash flow techniques using financial data, to customer-based corporate valuation (CBCV). Big data allows an immediate richness and superior predictability of the customer base health and progress. It also improves understanding and predictability of cash flow. It makes perfect sense that the value of an enterprise depends on what customers are spending, whether the customer base is growing and where the spending patterns are taking it. Before online connectivity gave us big data, however, it was impossible to put into place this kind of connection between customer data and corporate valuation.

The C-suite also needs a strong analytics function to optimize relationshipping spend, to predict where the customer base is growing and to understand the end goal of what this does to the valuation of the enterprise.

PRIVACY

Rarely does a day go by without news on the privacy front. There will be more legislation coming on this front. My suggestion: Manage your brand privacy with great care, transparency and sensitivity. Let your customers control their data, and reward them for it.

CONCLUSION

We are living through a dramatic pace of change brought about by the technology revolution. It is having a profound impact on the enterprises and brands that are advancing — and those that are declining.

My call to all — from those teaching marketing in our educational institutions (especially business schools), to all in the business community who are still using marketing to bring their brand, products and services to consumers — is this: Update. The new, more sophisticated, more informed discipline calls for relationshipping. I encourage you to update from the old Five Ps of marketing, and put the new Eight Ps of relationshipping in place.

CHAPTER 9
COMPANY CHANGES NEEDED FOR RELATIONSHIPPING

As of this writing, the number of enterprises in the Fortune 2000 that have embraced customer-centricity and re-organized around this principle has not quite reached 20%. Most enterprises are still aggressively siloed — with the website managed by IT, the advertising wrangled by the marketing group (along with an advertising agency), PR tended to by the public relations director and an agency, and digital efforts managed across separate agencies and programmatic providers, search providers, paid social providers, with retail and the call center isolated from all other communications. Meanwhile, it is not uncommon for product management to remain poorly plugged into all the prospect and customer contact interactions, resulting in limited visibility of brand and product engagement.

The street language for unifying these initiatives across a customer-centric approach: Connect the dots. As a CEO since 1976, I have learned that siloing corporate functions into focused departments has remained a tried-and-true way to control and operate an enterprise. The challenge, then, is how to take down silo walls and unify the brand and enterprise in a customer-centric, dot-connected configuration? We must do so while keeping the controls that C-titles want — especially those of the CEO and CFO. We cannot lose control of our enterprise in an attempt to connect the dots and still deliver a consistent, successful brand experience.

As marketing evolves into relationshipping, and traditional enterprise valuation is shifts toward customer-based corporate valuation (CBCV), it is all the more vital to connect the dots between spends that build customer lifetime value (CLV) — and use the outcome measures for CBCV to predict how this drives enterprise value.

I suggest that the CMO drive the C-suite team to focus on this space. It's essential that the entire team be plugged into CLV, because relationshipping communications is just one set of spends and considerations that will serve to optimize CLV. Of course, CLV also depends on product management and satisfaction with the product. Sales (in retail, online or to business), fulfillment and customer service also make a significant contribution. In other words, customer experience across the enterprise contributes to CLV and involves the entire C-level team.

In the interest of consistency, the CMO should evolve to become the CRO (Chief Relationships Officer), whose duties expand to include unifying customer experience and working with all members of the C-suite. At its best, relationshipping is a team sport. The CRO should lead the focus on these metrics and results because brand relationshipping communications and measurement represent the heart of data-driven customer engagement. The brand conversation with prospects and customers resides at the center of the relationship as brands field more personalization, automated assistants and voice, with transactions recorded in the customer data platform (CDP). Managing the relationshipping measures of CLV and insights from the customer data will largely be the responsibility of the CRO, even as it is shared across the team.

These efforts are still in their infancy. To my knowledge, there is no enterprise that is truly connecting the dots between CLV and CBCV. As I mentioned, only about 20% of Fortune 2000 organizations are customer-centric and non-siloed. That in turn limits the number of enterprises with customer-centric, CLV-focused relationshipping spends. And it is even less likely that the Fortune 2000 have engaged resources like Theta Equity Partners or moved to CBCV methods of tracking and predicting enterprise valuation. As C-suites begin to discover and deploy the connection of relationshipping to corporate value, this practice will grow, joining (and possibly even replacing) traditional methods of determining corporate value.

One option is to bring together the CMO/CRO and the head of product management to manage product satisfaction and the CDP together. This duo can then lead the process in the C-Suite to unite the functional areas in order to deliver a uniform brand experience with a focus on optimal CLV results.

Let's break it down further. Central to brand and enterprise success are product satisfaction and a growing customer base value. It's common sense, then, that Product Management and Relationshipping should be joined at the hip as technology enables product and brand personalization.

Only one thing stands between this effort: siloing. The product manager should collaborate closely with the CRO, sharing all satisfaction scores and product research. In turn, the CRO must incorporate all product attributes and experience issues, questions and ideas into regular LaunchPad-type measures. The CRO also needs to allow the PM visibility into the latest marketing results and CLV impact, while the PM shares thinking and direction on product development. This will optimize investment in product while simultaneously teeing up the best way to bring the product to customers and prospects.

Once this tight collaboration is in place, there needs to be a regular C-suite meeting (at least monthly) to get leadership aligned on a customer-centric focus. The goal: a unified customer experience that produces an optimized CLV.

The next step is to have regular reviews of forecasts from the CBCV models reflecting change in corporate value one year out, using the latest CLV metrics. It is important for the entire C-suite to see and discuss corporate value — whether it is moving up, moving down or remaining flat. The team will want to address what is working to drive corporate value up, and enhance those efforts. And obviously, any declines would need to be analyzed and addressed with new strategies and tactics.

Throughout my business courses, it was always a given that the main objective of the CEO and his or her team was to build corporate value. Without growth and returns, it cannot and does not work. My mission going forward is to help C-suites connect the dots, growing customer and corporate value. If we can do that successfully and consistently, all stakeholders will benefit.

Printed in the United States
By Bookmasters